I Am Kind

by Jenny Fretland VanVoorst

BLASTOFF! READERS

BELLWETHER MEDIA • MINNEAPOLIS, MN

Note to Librarians, Teachers, and Parents:

Blastoff! Readers are carefully developed by literacy experts and combine standards-based content with developmentally appropriate text.

Level 1 provides the most support through repetition of high-frequency words, light text, predictable sentence patterns, and strong visual support.

Level 2 offers early readers a bit more challenge through varied simple sentences, increased text load, and less repetition of high-frequency words.

Level 3 advances early-fluent readers toward fluency through increased text and concept load, less reliance on visuals, longer sentences, and more literary language.

Level 4 builds reading stamina by providing more text per page, increased use of punctuation, greater variation in sentence patterns, and increasingly challenging vocabulary.

Level 5 encourages children to move from "learning to read" to "reading to learn" by providing even more text, varied writing styles, and less familiar topics.

Whichever book is right for your reader, Blastoff! Readers are the perfect books to build confidence and encourage a love of reading that will last a lifetime!

This edition first published in 2019 by Bellwether Media, Inc.

No part of this publication may be reproduced in whole or in part without written permission of the publisher. For information regarding permission, write to Bellwether Media, Inc., Attention: Permissions Department, 6012 Blue Circle Drive, Minnetonka, MN 55343.

Library of Congress Cataloging-in-Publication Data

Names: Fretland VanVoorst, Jenny, 1972- author.
Title: I Am Kind / by Jenny Fretland VanVoorst.
Description: Minneapolis, MN : Bellwether Media, Inc., 2019. |
   Series: Blastoff! Readers: Character Education | Includes bibliographical references and index.
Identifiers: LCCN 2018033437 (print) | LCCN 2018034231 (ebook) |
   ISBN 9781681036533 (ebook) | ISBN 9781626179288 (hardcover : alk. paper) |
   ISBN 9781618914996 (pbk. : alk. paper)
Subjects: LCSH: Kindness–Juvenile literature.
Classification: LCC BJ1533.K5 (ebook) | LCC BJ1533.K5 F74 2019 (print) | DDC 177/.7–dc23
LC record available at https://lccn.loc.gov/2018033437

Editor: Christina Leaf   Designer: Jeffrey Kollock

Printed in the United States of America, North Mankato, MN

Table of Contents

What Is Kindness?

Your sister falls
and hurts her knee.
She has tears
in her eyes.

Do you still play?
Or do you
comfort her?

Kind people care about others.
They think about how others might feel.

Kind people
comfort and help.
They listen and **share**.

Kind people treat everyone well. They are nice to others. They are nice to themselves!

Why Be Kind?

Kindness helps build good **relationships**. People like others who make them feel good.

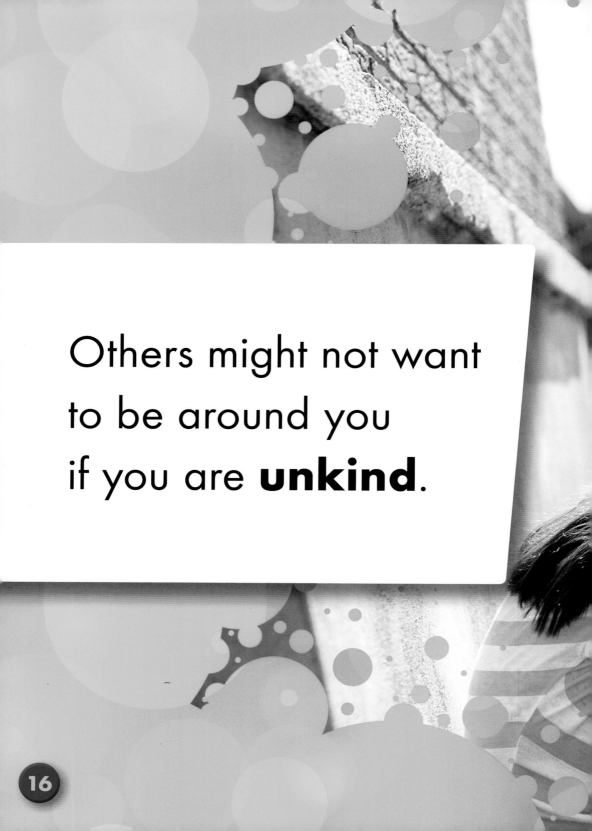

Others might not want
to be around you
if you are **unkind**.

You Are Kind!

It is easy to be kind. Treat others how you would like to be treated.

Who Is Kind?

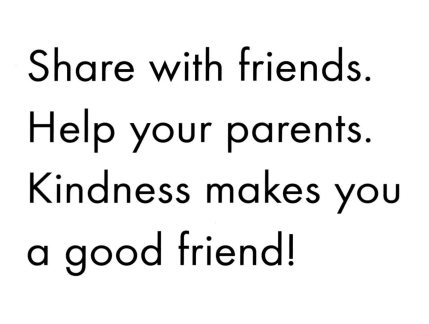

Share with friends. Help your parents. Kindness makes you a good friend!

Glossary

comfort

to help a person who is sad, hurt, or in trouble

share

to use and enjoy something with others

relationships

ties with other people

unkind

not nice to others

To Learn More

AT THE LIBRARY

Kalban, Rachel. *Daniel Chooses to Be Kind*. New York, N.Y.: Simon Spotlight, 2017.

Miller, Pat Zietlow. *Be Kind*. New York, N.Y.: Roaring Brook Press, 2018.

Shepherd, Jodie. *Kindness and Generosity: It Starts with Me*. New York, N.Y.: Scholastic Children's Press, 2016.

ON THE WEB

FACTSURFER

Factsurfer.com gives you a safe, fun way to find more information.

1. Go to www.factsurfer.com.

2. Enter "kind" into the search box.

3. Click the "Surf" button and select your book cover to see a list of related web sites.

Index

The images in this book are reproduced through the courtesy of: Africa Studio, front cover; John T, pp. 2-3, 22-24; MNStudio, pp. 4-5, 6-7; fstop123, pp. 8-9; FatCamera, pp. 10-11, 19 (bad); Robert Kneschke, pp. 12-13, 20-21; Rawpixel.com, pp. 14-15; Lopolo, pp. 16-17; kali9, pp. 18-19; Monkey Business Images, pp. 19 (good), 22 (top right); unguryanu, p. 22 (top left); Sergey Novikov, p. 22 (middle left); gpointstudio, p. 22 (middle right).